This book belongs to

Egyptians

Stephanie Turnbull

Designed by Laura Parker

Illustrated by Colin King

Cover illustration by Ian Jackson

Additional illustrations by Tim Haggerty

Egypt consultant: Miriam Bibby

Reading consultant: Alison Kelly,
Roehampton University

Contents

People of the past

Egypt is a hot country in north Africa. The people who lived there thousands of years ago are called ancient Egyptians.

This picture is part of an ancient Egyptian wall painting. It shows a group of servants.

Egyptian paintings often show things from the side.

River life

The ancient Egyptians built their towns and cities along a river called the Nile.

This photograph of Egypt was taken from space. The river and its banks look dark green.

Red Sea

River Nile————

The yellow parts are dry, dusty deserts.

The Egyptians fished
in the river and
sailed boats on it.

They drank water
from it and used it
for washing clothes.

This is an ancient
Egyptian model
of a boat.

People swam in the Nile, but they
had to watch out for crocodiles.

Farmers

Egyptian farmers grew fruit, vegetables and other plants on the banks of the Nile.

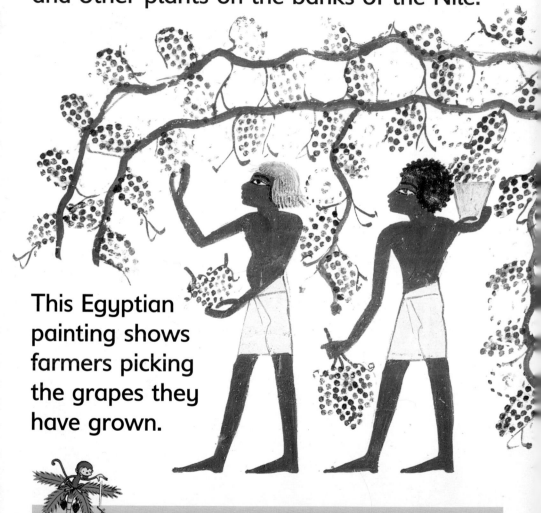

This Egyptian painting shows farmers picking the grapes they have grown.

Farmers trained monkeys to pick fruit from high trees and throw it down.

The Nile flooded every year. This made the soil good for growing plants.

When the land dried up, plants grew in the sun. Farmers worked hard in the fields.

Farmers kept some of the crops to eat, and took the rest to markets.

At home

Ancient Egyptian houses were made
of dried mud and painted white.

Houses had small windows to
keep out the hot sun.

People cooked food and
baked bread outside.

Some people had a
pool in their garden
where they kept
fish to eat.

Egyptians slept on hard wooden beds, with wooden headrests instead of pillows.

Rich people often had servants. This model shows servants hard at work baking bread.

Kings of Egypt

Egyptian kings were called pharaohs.
The pharaoh was the richest and most
important person in the whole country.

A pharaoh made
laws and gave orders.

He led his soldiers
to fight enemies.

He went out hunting
in his chariot.

He also met visitors
from other countries.

All pharaohs wore crowns. Some were decorated with gold and jewels.

This is a painting of Ramesses III. He is wearing a gold crown and a long, striped headdress.

Pharaoh Ramesses II had a pet lion to scare away enemies.

Gods and goddesses

Ancient Egyptians believed in many different gods and goddesses.

Egyptian gods sometimes looked like animals. This goddess, called Hathor, was often shown as a cow.

In this wall painting, Hathor has the horns of a cow on her crown.

Sekhmet was a fierce war goddess.

Ra was the powerful sun god.

Bes looked after children and families.

Ma'at was the goddess of truth.

Horus looked after pharaohs.

Seth was the evil uncle of Horus.

Horus and Seth were enemies. They once turned into fierce hippos to fight.

Temples

The Egyptians built huge stone temples to worship pharaohs and gods.

This is the temple of Pharaoh Ramesses II. Each statue outside the temple is more than ten times taller than a person.

In a temple, priests prayed to a statue of a god or pharaoh.

On special days, they carried the statue through the town.

This is a statue of Anubis, a god who could change into an animal called a jackal.

People often had small statues of gods at home, too.

Making a mummy

When an important person died, Egyptians wrapped their body so it didn't rot. This is called making a mummy.

1. First they took out the person's insides and put them in pots.

2. Then they packed the body in salt to dry it out.

3. Next, they wrapped the body tightly in bandages.

4. Finally, they put a mask on the mummy and laid it in a coffin.

Egyptians made
animal mummies too.

The person's insides
were kept in pots with
lids like these. Each
pot has a god's head.

Coffins were shaped to look like a person
and covered with spells and pictures.

Giant pyramids

When a pharaoh died, his coffin was put inside an enormous stone pyramid.

These large pyramids were built for three different pharaohs. The smaller pyramids were for their families.

Workers cut stone blocks and dragged them along.

They pulled the blocks up a ramp, onto the pyramid.

18

After many years of work, they put the last stone on top.

Finally, workers made the pyramid smooth and shiny.

Underground tombs

After many years, Egyptians stopped building pyramids. They buried important people in underground tombs instead.

1. First, workers dug a deep tunnel into a rocky cliff.

2. Then they built rooms and corridors underground.

3. They painted the walls and filled the rooms with treasure.

4. They put the coffin inside a huge box in a special room.

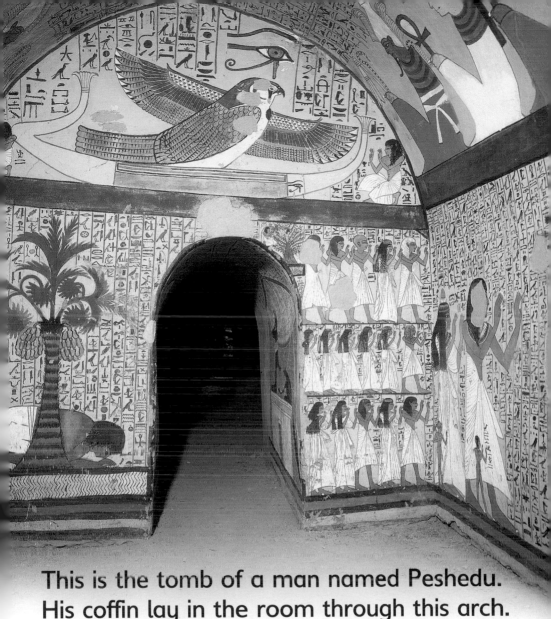

This is the tomb of a man named Peshedu.
His coffin lay in the room through this arch.

Robbers often dug into tombs
and pyramids to steal treasure.

Hidden treasure

The tomb of the pharaoh Tutankhamun was hidden for thousands of years.

In 1922, explorers found a secret door, hidden behind rocks.

Inside were rooms crammed with glittering treasure.

It took ten years to clear the tomb and list all the amazing treasures.

This falcon was one of the many beautiful statues in the tomb.

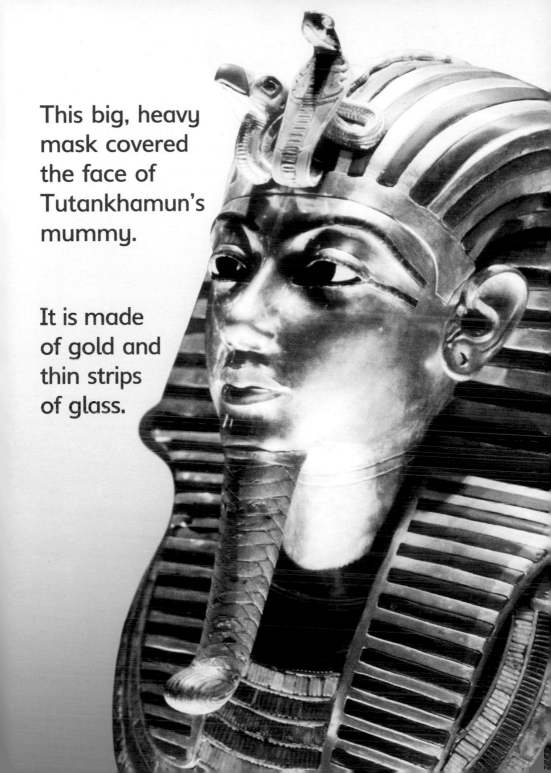

This big, heavy
mask covered
the face of
Tutankhamun's
mummy.

It is made
of gold and
thin strips
of glass.

Fun and games

Egyptians loved sports and games, as well as music, dancing and parties.

Some people learned to play instruments, like this harp.

Men liked to have boating contests on the River Nile.

The team that pushed the other boat over won the game.

This painting shows a man hunting with his family. He is standing on a boat and throwing a stick at birds.

At parties, people enjoyed watching dancers perform all kinds of difficult moves.

Dressing up

Egyptians liked to look good. They wore simple, flowing clothes and lots of jewels.

This wide,
gold necklace is
shaped like a bird.
It was made for
a pharaoh.

People often put perfumed fat on their heads. As it melted, it made them smell nice.

Men and women wore loose, light skirts and dresses that kept them cool.

They decorated the clothes with rings, bracelets, necklaces and other jewels.

Everyone wore make-up too. They put lots of dark paint around their eyes.

Most people shaved their heads to keep cool. Adults usually wore wigs.

Egyptian writing

Egyptian writing was made up of lots of pictures called hieroglyphs.

People called scribes could read and write hieroglyphs. The statue below shows a scribe.

A scribe's job was to write letters and keep records.

He also had to teach children to read and write.

These hieroglyphs were painted on a tomb.
They are spells to protect a dead person.

Most ordinary people didn't have
a clue what hieroglyphs meant.

Glossary of Egyptian words

Here are some of the words in this book you might not know. This page tells you what they mean.

 pharaoh - the title ancient Egyptians gave their king.

 temple - a place where Egyptians went to worship gods and dead pharaohs.

 priest - a person who worked in a temple. Priests prayed to statues.

 mummy - a body that has been dried out to make it last for many years.

 tomb - a place under the ground where a person was buried.

 scribe - a person whose job was to read and write.

 hieroglyph - a picture or symbol. Egyptians wrote using hieroglyphs.

Websites to visit

If you have a computer, you can find out more about ancient Egyptians on the Internet. On the Usborne Quicklinks Website there are links to four fun websites.

Website 1 - Play an Egyptian board game with a friend.

Website 2 - See your name in hieroglyphs.

Website 3 - Read about lots of different gods and goddesses.

Website 4 - Print out Egyptian pictures to crayon.

To visit these websites, go to **www.usborne-quicklinks.com** Read the Internet safety guidelines, and then type the keywords "beginners egyptians".

The websites are regularly reviewed and the links in Usborne Quicklinks are updated. However, Usborne Publishing is not responsible, and does not accept liability, for the content or availability of any website other than its own. We recommend that children are supervised while on the Internet.

Index

Acknowledgements

Photographic manipulation by Emma Julings

Photo credits
The publishers are grateful to the following for permission to reproduce material:
© **Alamy** 18–19, 31 (Brian Lawrence); © **The Ancient Art and Architecture Collection Ltd** 12;
© **The Art Archive** 17b (Musée du Louvre Paris/Dagli Orti); © **Copyright The British Museum** 5, 17t, 24;
© **Corbis** 2–3, 6, 9, 21 (all Gianni Dagli Orti), 1, 15, 22 (all Sandro Vannini), 25 (Archivo Iconografico, S.A.),
26 (Bettman), 28 (Roger Wood), 29 (Wolfgang Kaehler); © **Digital Vision** back cover;
© **Getty Images** 14 (Richard Passmore), 23 (Alvis Upitis); © **Heritage Images**
11 (The British Library); © **NASA** 4 (Jacques Descloitres, MODIS Land Science Team)

Every effort has been made to trace and acknowledge ownership of copyright. If any rights have
been omitted, the publishers offer to rectify this in any subsequent editions following notification.

Vikings

Castles

How flowers grow

Knights

Living in space

Caterpillars and Butterflies

Ballet

Pirates

Egyptians

Eggs and Chicks

Romans

Dinosaurs

Tadpoles and frogs

Why do we eat?

Under the sea

Weather